Ashton!

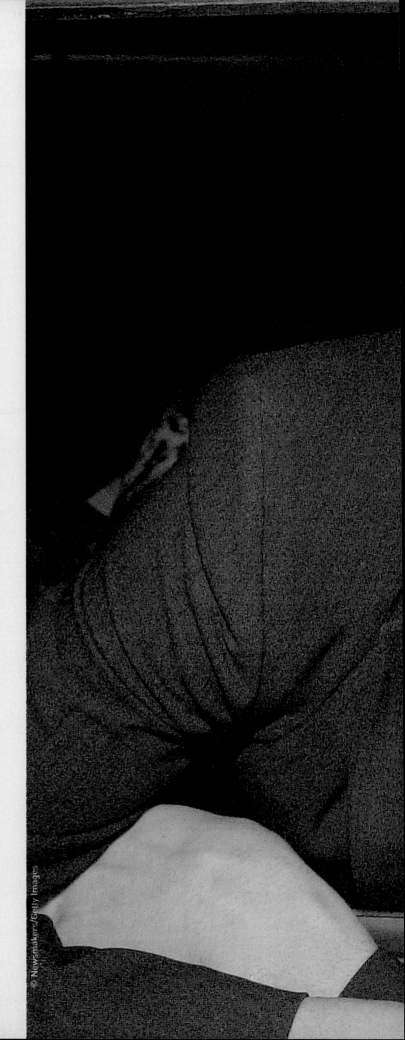

SIMON SPOTLIGHT
An imprint of Simon & Schuster
Children's Publishing Division
1230 Avenue of the Americas
New York, New York, 10020

SIMON SPOTLIGHT is a trademark
of Simon & Schuster, Inc.

Designed by Ann Sullivan

Printed in the United States of America
First Edition

10 9 8 7 6 5 4 3 2 1

ISBN 0-689-86780-8

© Newsmakers/Getty Images

Grace Norwich

Ashton!

SIMON SPOTLIGHT™

New York   London   Toronto   Sydney   Singapore

ASHTON KUTCHER

has always been into pranks. Way before his hit MTV show *Punk'd*, in which he plays outrageous tricks on unsuspecting celebrities, Ashton came up with unusual ways to entertain himself in his tiny hometown of Homestead, Iowa. But unlike the elaborate jokes he plays now for MTV, his earlier stunts didn't always turn out so funny.

When Ashton was a senior at Clear Creek Amana High School, he and his cousin broke into the school to steal money out of the soda machine for kicks. Even though Ashton easily picked the school's locks, the burglars encountered something they hadn't prepared for: a silent alarm in the library. They were nabbed by the cops and thrown in jail. Ashton's stepdad Mark Portwood had warned the troublemaker before: If Ashton were ever sent to jail, he would have to stay there. Sure enough, Mark remained true to his word. When Ashton called his stepdad from jail that night, Mark told him to have a good night and hung up the phone. In addition to an uncomfortable night in a jail cell, Ashton's bad behavior made him lose out on an acting part: the role of

1

Ashton, with former flame Brittany Murphy, met pal Sean "P. Diddy" Combs at an NBA All-Star Game.

Daddy Warbucks in the school production of *Annie*, for which he had already shaved his head.

He may never regain the chance to play Daddy Warbucks (although Ashton wants to go bald again and has tried to convince the creators of *That '70s Show* to send his character Michael Kelso to the army so he can shave his head), but today the twenty-five-year-old star is one of the hottest actors working in Hollywood. In 2003 he was named one of *E! Online*'s Twenty-Five Most Eligible Bachelors and *People* magazine's Fifty Most Beautiful People. How did Ashton go in only a few years from partying with pals around bonfires in the cornfields of Iowa to running up a

Ashton at the premiere of *Just Married*

four-thousand-dollar restaurant bill when he dined out with Puff Daddy and friends? A naturally outgoing person, Ashton has always loved to perform. Steve Weiss, an acting teacher from Ashton's school days, recognized that his student would go far beyond the Old Creamery Theater in Amana. "Sometimes you spot someone, and you know that person could go on to really be something," Steve told the *Des Moines Register*. "I think he had it."

With his strong 6'3" frame, chiseled jaw, large brown eyes, and beautifully long double row of eyelashes, which he names as his best feature, Ashton stands out from the crowd. But what makes him special, or really "something," as his teacher Steve put it, stems from more than just his looks. Both on-screen and off, Ashton is fun loving and full of energy. He

is known for the goofy, airheaded characters he plays, such as on *That '70s Show* or in the films *Dude, Where's My Car?* and *Just Married.* In real life, Ashton is anything but stupid. Danny Masterson, who plays Steven Hyde on *That '70s Show*, quickly discovered that his costar, once a biochemical engineering student in college, is no dummy. "We found out how smart he was when we were sitting around talking about high school science," Danny says. "He started rattling off stuff about chemicals and the body." He's cute, smart, and a self-professed hard worker, but perhaps Ashton's best qualities are his good attitude and low-key nature.

He has all the accoutrements of a big star—a house in Los Angeles, a

Ashton with *That '70s Show* costar Danny Masterson

Signing autographs at the premiere of *Dude, Where's My Car?*

Land Rover, courtside seats at Lakers games, millions of fans, and a big paycheck—but he still hasn't forgotten his heartland roots. Back in Homestead, where he likes to go fishing when he visits, he says his family doesn't put too much stock in his fame. "It's a job," says Ashton, who always makes a point of going home for the holidays. "They know that. They understand that. If I ever went home with a big head, I'd get put in my place so fast—they'd have me outside shoveling the roof."

The down-to-earth star has real all-American roots. Christopher Ashton Kutcher was born on February 7, 1978, in Cedar Rapids, Iowa. His fraternal twin, Michael, was born five minutes after Ashton, and the two are as close as their birth times. "He's more outgoing and energetic than I am," says Michael, who works in the banking industry. "He always stood up for me." The brothers have a sister, Tausha, who is three years older.

Ashton poses with his mom, Diane . . .

Ashton's parents both worked in factories while he was growing up. His mother Diane, whom he describes as "the strongest person I know," worked on the Head & Shoulders assembly line and brought home free products from the Procter & Gamble factory. Ashton would just grab whatever soap or shampoo was available in the shower, and he pretty much sticks to the same effortless beauty regimen today. "I

. . . and shares a laugh with his father, Larry.

don't use lotions or fancy shampoos," he told *People* magazine. "I was never picky about that stuff. So why start changing things now?" His dad, Larry, worked on the Fruit Roll-Ups line for General Mills. While on summer vacation from college, Ashton worked at the same plant, where he earned twelve dollars an hour sweeping up heavy Cheerios dust. Although it wasn't exactly a glamorous job, Ashton loved it so much that he says, "I was singing as I swept up that dust."

Larry and Diane divorced, but Ashton doesn't have bitter feelings about his parents' split. "My parents are so cool," he said to *Rolling Stone*. "They couldn't have handled it better." The real trauma of his childhood came when Ashton was thirteen. His brother, Michael, had an emergency heart transplant after he had contracted cardiomyopathy, a viral heart inflammation that sent him into cardiac arrest. "They gave him about six hours to live and then they found a new heart for him," recalls Ashton, who says he would have donated his own heart to his twin. "My brother is my hero. If he can survive that, I can do any-thing." During that experience Ashton never left his brother's side. "A

lot of people see the wit about Ashton, but they don't see the sensitive side," Diane says. "He's got a big heart."

A couple of years after Michael's transplant, Diane and Ashton's stepfather, Mark, a construction worker, moved the family to a three-hundred-acre farm near Homestead, a town with a population of one hundred. As a teenager, Ashton engaged in activities like sports and hunting, and he was even part of his school's choir. Aside from the occasional keg party in the cornfields, the small-town atmosphere of Homestead made it difficult for Ashton to get into any real trouble. "The worst thing was that in my town, everyone had a police scanner, and for kicks they'd sit around and listen to who was getting in trouble," he told *Cosmopolitan*. "My parents knew if I'd been caught speeding before I even walked in the door."

Most people now know Ashton as a confident, broad-shouldered movie star with beautiful women by his side. But at Clear Creek Amana High School, where he was in a graduating class of fifty-four students, he wasn't particularly studly. During his freshman year, he was rather gangly, weighing in at only 103 pounds. Years after high school, Ashton relived his geeky past on the set of *Dude, Where's My Car?* when he discovered that the high school girl of his dreams was also in the movie. "Kristy Swanson was like a goddess," he says. "No other girl was in her league." The two had a make-out scene, but Ashton blew it. "I got so worked up, I shot a breath out of my nose that was kind of like a snort, and snot came flying out onto her," he says, laughing. "I blew snot on my dream goddess girl!"

Ashton's high energy propelled him to participate in almost every extracurricular activity in high school. Besides choir, wrestling, football, and track, he was also a member of the National Honor Society. So it

Ashton gets back to his heartland roots at a 2002 Halloween party.

Ashton with Sean William Scott

wasn't surprising when he entered the University of Iowa, not far from home, in 1995 to study biochemical engineering. His plan was to become a geneticist so that he could try to find a cure for his brother's disease. Ashton engrossed himself in the heady world of double helixes and RNA regulation. Still, he knew he wanted to be somewhere else, somewhere other than Iowa.

Ashton at a benefit for Multiple Sclerosis

3 1833 04503 2130

Luckily for him fate was waiting for him in the form of a talent scout at The Airliner, a restaurant and bar in Iowa City. During final exams in the fall of 1996, Ashton was hanging out with a group of his friends when Mary Brown, a modeling agent based out of Cedar Rapids, approached him. Mary knew a good thing when she saw it—Ashton's corn-fed good looks, with that hint of mischievousness, were the qualities all the top designers wanted in a model. When she suggested that he give modeling a shot, Ashton was dubious. Was she scamming him? When he thought of models, he pictured people very different from himself. Frankly he pictured Cindy Crawford. "I thought Fabio was the only male model. Then I realized, oh, the Marlboro Man isn't really a cowboy. So I thought I'd give it a shot," he says.

Ashton put his skepticism aside, entered the 1997 Fresh Face of Iowa modeling contest, and won a trip to New York City. Two days after he arrived in the big city, he had landed a spot at the prestigious modeling agency Next and was already getting jobs. Soon he was commanding two thousand dollars a day, a sum he never could have conceived of earning when he was sweeping up Cheerios dust. Hanging out with friends among the haystacks of Iowa quickly became a distant memory. He began traveling the world to walk the catwalks of such European cities as Milan and Paris, and appeared on gigantic billboards in advertisements for Calvin Klein. Ashton marveled at his good fortune. Modeling was a lot easier than most of his summer jobs. "All I had to do," he says about the runway shows, "was walk from here to the door and back."

In 1998, after a year of having his image splashed across billboards and magazines, Ashton headed for Hollywood. Although his only experience with acting had been in school, it was a natural leap for someone

Ashton got his start modeling in 1997.

with such innate charisma and magnetism. The first play he ever did was *The Crying Princess and the Golden Goose* in seventh grade. In high school he was a member of the Thespian Society and snagged the lead in *To Kill a Mockingbird.* But it wasn't until he tired of modeling that he really considered pursuing a career in acting.

Ashton arrived in Los Angeles to audition for *Wind on Water*, an NBC

cowboy-surfer show that starred Bo Derek. Despite getting the part right away, he also auditioned for Fox's *That '70s Show*, which follows the adventures of a group of Wisconsin teens coming of age in the disco era. Immediately after trying out for the role of the loveable space cadet, Michael Kelso, he told the creators he needed to find out whether or not he got the part by 3:45 P.M. because the folks at NBC were expecting an answer to their offer by 4:00 P.M. They made the quick yet wise decision to hire Ashton. Bonnie Turner, cocreator of *That '70s Show*, explains that he got the role because "everyone else was reading the character as stupid, but Ashton made him naive." Plus, she says, "He knocked us all out

The "Teenage Millionaire" (left) rocks some very '70s shades (above).

Friends—both on-screen and off

with the way he looked." Whatever the reason, Ashton says, "It was a blessing in disguise. . . . Well, not really in disguise. It was just a blessing."

Not everything went smoothly on the show at first. Right after they finished the pilot, the cast assembled on a trampoline for a publicity photo shoot, where Ashton tried to entertain his costars by pulling some fancy moves. "I used to be able to do back flips, but I must have jumped wrong because I flew off it and wrecked a wall on the set by going through it," he told *Teen People*. Back flips were not the only area in his life that needed improvement; acting was also on his list of new challenges.

Ashton, who says he is not naturally funny, except for the way his legs

Ashton goofs around with Wilmer Valderrama and Mila Kunis.

look, thought he was going to be fired after the first five episodes of the Fox show. "I was so terrible," he recalls. While he did have things to learn, so did the rest of the cast. Nobody on the show was born before 1976 and they all needed a little tutorial on what life was like back in the seventies. They watched *The Brady Bunch* and read old magazines. "I knew you didn't talk back to your parents then," Ashton reasons. "They could beat their kids without going to jail." The other actors on the show, like Topher Grace, Laura Prepon, and Mila Kunis, bonded with Ashton over more than bell-bottoms and lava lamps. "Those guys are my best friends," says Ashton, who goes dancing and bowling with his TV buddies, or has them over to his house to play pool. "How are you going to beat a job where you go and hang out with your friends all week and then

on Friday somehow you make a TV show? And you make people laugh for a living. That's a great job." The chemistry the young actors share also comes through in their performances on the show and has turned the sitcom into a longstanding hit. Ashton's family members are counted among the show's many fans. Michael especially approves of his brother's performance. "Watching *That '70s Show*," he says, "you're getting pure Ashton."

Ashton has since settled into life in Los Angeles. He lives in a house with his good friend and personal assistant, T. J. Jefferson, his black lab, Willy Wonka, and his golden retriever, Mr. Bojangles. There is always plenty of action happening at the Kutcher household. Between the tennis court and the pool, it's the ultimate bachelor pad that lots of girls would no doubt like to visit. While Ashton says having people he doesn't know in his home "freaks him out," he made an exception for the presidential twins. He had the Bush girls, Jenna and Barbara, over to hang out after they met one night at a party. Ashton is convinced that his phone has been tapped by the Secret Service ever since.

Between parties Ashton works on fixing up his place. His choice of decor includes memorabilia from *The Shawshank Redemption*, one of his favorite movies, and from Walter Payton, one of his favorite football players. He also put some of his own elbow grease into renovating his house. Using the carpentry skills he picked up in Iowa, Ashton built a new deck. Although he could have easily paid someone else to do it, he enlisted the help of ten of his friends in painting his floor in exchange for free beer. "He's always randomly building stuff," says Mila, who was invited over with other cast mates from *That '70s Show* to see the new deck. "That's what he's like—very levelheaded."

Ashton has always had a thrifty, survivalist streak, even when it

Ashton at a 2003 Super Bowl party in San Diego

© Tammie Arroyo / Retna Ltd. USA

comes to clothes. While growing up, the cool rich kids wore Ralph Lauren Polo shirts, but Ashton tried to get by with a low-priced Knights of the Round Table shirt. It was not unlike the popular brand-name Polo in that it featured a man on a horse, but Ashton explains, "He was carrying a flag. I had one of those shirts, and I tried to pull out a little thread to make the flag look like a polo stick so I wouldn't get ribbed." These days the hard-working actor doesn't have to worry about the price of his wardrobe, or whether his clothes are cool enough. His closet is filled with Armani, Gucci, and Calvin Klein for more formal occasions, and he likes Levi's and Nike when dressing casually. He always wears what he calls the "urban casual tie" to work—that is, he wears a tie with a short-sleeved shirt. "It's a way to keep things in perspective," Ashton told *InStyle*. "Acting can be so much fun that it's easy to forget that what you're doing is a job. But if I've got my tie on, I'm going to work." The one thing about his job on *That '70s Show* that bums him out is the shaggy David Cassidy–style haircut he has to sport. Not one to fuss over

Ashton poses with pals Mila Kunis and Danny Masterson.

his hair, he says, "I'd probably shave my head so I wouldn't have to deal with it. To me, as a guy, hair is just the most senseless thing in the world."

The girls in Ashton's life might not feel the same way he does about doing away with his adorably scruffy locks. Although he claims that he was an awkward guy who didn't have a girlfriend until his senior year in high school, it's hard to believe that Ashton ever had a problem with women. Mila, who plays his TV girlfriend, understands what women see in her costar: his lips, eyes, bone structure, and toned body. "He's a hottie," she says. He's also head-over-heels for the opposite sex. "I get really giddy and stupid with girls," he told *Rolling Stone.* "I love the company of women. I fall in love superfast, and I'll want to spend the next week together, twenty-four hours a day. I will drop everything when it's

The former model looks as good in Gucci as he does in Levi's.

starting, and that's stupid. If you're not going to take a week off on a regular basis, don't do it in the beginning."

Ashton met his first long-term girlfriend, actress January Jones, when he was still modeling. The two were on a photo shoot for an Abercrombie & Fitch catalog and became good friends. About a year later, Ashton went to New York and asked if he could "crash at her pad." After that the two were together. He says, "Basically I never left." At the time of the romance, he described what made them such a good couple. "What keeps it going is that we're such good friends," he told *Cosmopolitan.* "So even if we get in a fight, we'll hate each other for a day, but then the next day, we fall in

Ashton cracking up with Ashley Scott

love all over again." After their breakup, January Jones was a bit less resilient, and told *People* magazine, "Romance is too hard in this town." Ashton dated his next girlfriend, Ashley Scott, the star of the short-lived WB action series *Birds of Prey*, for nine months before they split.

When he began shooting his romantic comedy *Just Married* with Brittany Murphy, Ashton was still dating Ashley. But he had instant chemistry with his new costar, who was just coming off a reported romance with *8 Mile* star Eminem. As they filmed in some of Europe's

Ashton met January Jones on a photo shoot.

most romantic cities, he and Brittany grew closer. On breaks from film-ing, the two goofed off together, often jabbering away in a made-up version of Italian. Many people questioned if they were even acting dur-ing their scenes, but both swear up and down that they didn't get together until after the film wrapped. The couple announced that they were together in October 2002 and kicked off the news with heavy make-out sessions from coast to coast as they promoted their film.

Ashton and Brittany made a funny pair because of their drastic height difference—he's 6'3" and she's 5'1"—but he was smitten. "I like every-thing about her," he told *People* magazine. "She's just the total package."

Ashton and Brittany greet fans at the VH1 Big in 2002 Awards.

The two, who enjoyed eating sushi and going to the drive-in theater in Pasadena, were not totally unlike the bumbling couple they play in *Just Married*. Once they fell asleep with a candle still burning, and Brittany's purse caught on fire. Ashton hopped out of bed and fought the four-foot flames shooting off his dresser. Height differences and fire disasters aside, they seemed to be a good fit for each other. He brought her home to meet his parents. She gave him a diamond-studded cross pendant for

Despite the high heels, Brittany Murphy barely reaches Ashton's shoulders.

ASHTON!

25

Ashton with Demi Moore and family at the *Charlie's Angels: Full Throttle* premiere

Christmas. Still, Ashton and Brittany's romance petered out after seven months.

In May 2003 Ashton's love life again made headlines when his romance with forty-year-old actress Demi Moore surfaced. The pair stirred up quite a tabloid frenzy when they were spotted on a romantic weekend getaway in Miami. After a number of sightings around Los Angeles, Ashton and Demi finally made their relationship public at the premiere of Demi's comeback film *Charlie's Angels: Full Throttle*, where they were joined by her three daughters and ex-husband Bruce Willis.

But whatever his relationships of the moment may be, Ashton's major

Ashton with friend and *Punk'd* victim Justin Timberlake

love is his MTV show, *Punk'd*, created with Jason Goldberg. According to Ashton, the point of the show "is to have someone throw a punch or start crying." With characteristic zeal for a good prank, Ashton has thrown himself into this job heart and soul. Top celebrities like Justin Timberlake, who was led to believe that tax enforcers were seizing all of his belongings, or Jack Osbourne, who was asked to strip down to his underwear in order to pass MTV's building security, have been put through Ashton's twisted plots. No one seems to hold it against him, not even tough New Yorker Rosario Dawson, who was picked up by an offensive limo driver who committed a fake hit-and-run with her in the car.

Even though he loves entertaining millions by making fun of famous people, Ashton wants to shed his *Dude, Where's My Car?* image and star

in more serious films, like the psychological thriller *The Butterfly Effect*, which is his first attempt at the darker side of film. Whatever the medium, whether zany, romantic, or somber, Ashton will continue to show up in magazines, television, and film for some time to come. That's because his work keeps him going. "I'm very awkward when I have time off," he told *USA Today*. "I don't know what to do with myself. It's weird not to work."

That's exactly what Hollywood producers and his fans want to hear, but with Ashton anything is possible. The young actor has said he only has ten years left in him before he'll retire from show business. "I want to be a full-time student and just study and learn, and be a father and settle down. When I have kids I'll be a full-time father," he explains. "That's my intention anyway."